Kindergarten Countdown

written by
ANNA JANE HAYS

illustrated by
LINDA DAVICK

Alfred A. Knopf 🐕 New York

For Lucy,
with love
—A.J.H.

To my mom,
who sent me
to Miss Kay's
—L.D.

THIS IS A BORZOI BOOK
PUBLISHED BY ALFRED A. KNOPF
Text copyright © 2007 by Anna Jane Hays
Illustrations copyright © 2007 by Linda Davick
All rights reserved.
Published in the United States by Alfred A. Knopf,
an imprint of Random House Children's Books, a division
of Random House, Inc., New York.
KNOPF, BORZOI BOOKS, and the colophon are registered
trademarks of Random House, Inc.
www.randomhouse.com/kids
Educators and librarians, for a variety of teaching tools,
visit us at www.randomhouse.com/teachers
Library of Congress Control Number 2006024249
ISBN 978-0-375-84252-8 (trade) — ISBN 978-0-375-94252-5 (lib. bdg.)
The illustrations in this book were created using Adobe Illustrator
and Photoshop on an iBook G4.
MANUFACTURED IN MALAYSIA
July 2007 • 10 9 8 7 6 5 4 3 2 1 • First Edition

My school starts in one week, so—
I have seven days to go.
Mom says be patient, do not worry.
But I can't wait! I'm in a hurry!

7 days to Kindergarten.

I'll be ready, I'll be smart.
I will get a running start.
I'll say thank you,
I'll say please.
I will say
my ABCs!

Monday

6 days to Kindergarten.

I'll be ready,
I'll be good.
I will sit still
when I should.
I'll use a tissue
when I sneeze.
I will count
my 1-2-3's!

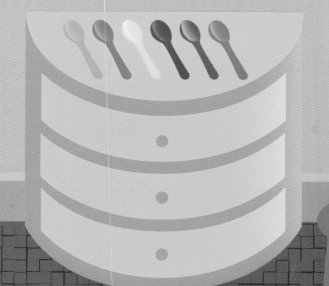

5 days to Kindergarten.

Yay!
Then I'll go to school
in flashy sneakers (oh so cool)!
I'll wear my superhero sweater
that makes me feel
strong and better.

Wednesday

4 days to Kindergarten.

I'm all set for show-and-tell
(and I can do it very well).
I'll bring my pokey little snail
and talk about his slimy trail.

Thursday

3 days to Kindergarten.

Three more days
and this week ends.
I can't wait
to make new friends!
We'll take turns
and play new games,
and practice writing
our own names.

2 days to Kindergarten.

Is it time to make my lunch?
Banana sandwich, ice cream crunch,
Popsicles, pickles, one lollipop.
At school I'll ask who wants to swap.

SCHOOL STARTS!

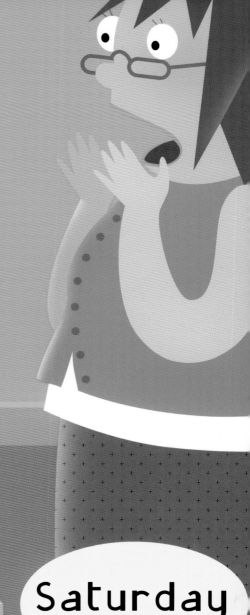

Saturday

1 day to Kindergarten.

Now it's time to pack my stuff.
Hope my backpack's big enough
for my picture book and truck
and shiny rock to bring me luck.

School is just
one night away!

I brush my teeth and jump in bed
with letters and numbers in my head.
I will try to go to sleep
by counting Kindergarten sheep!

O days to Kindergarten.

I waited seven days to say—

Kindergarten starts today!

Monday